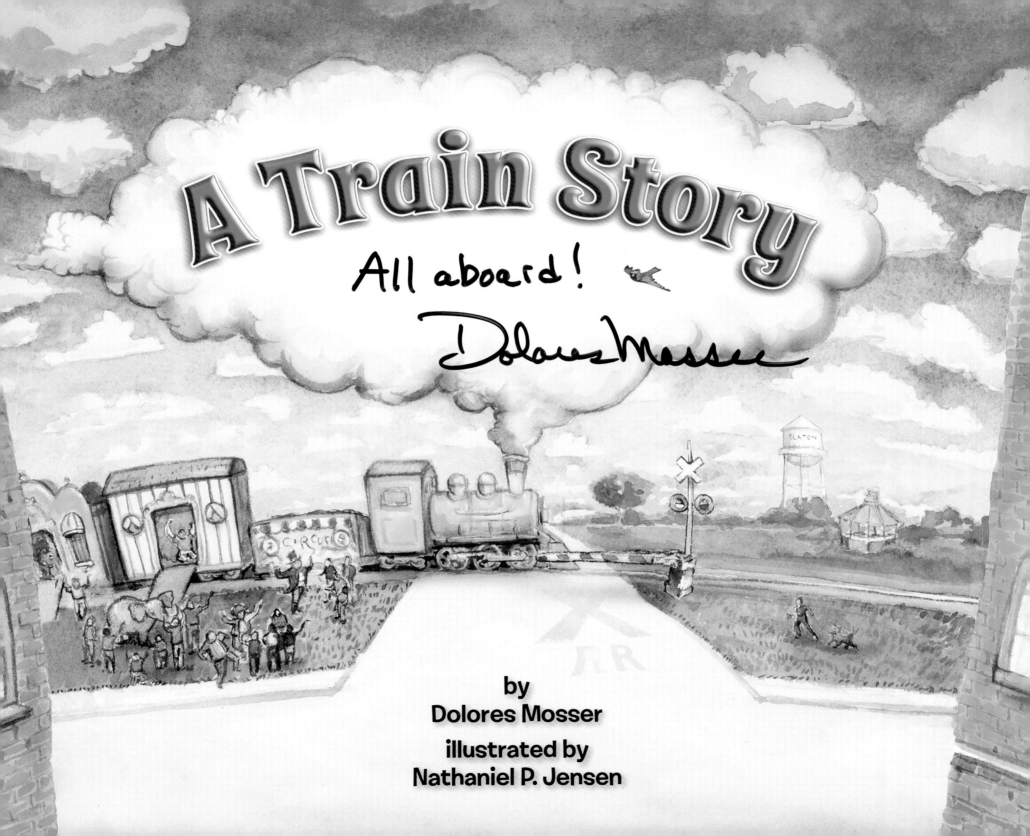

A Train Story

All aboard!

Dolores Mosser

by
Dolores Mosser

illustrated by
Nathaniel P. Jensen

Published and distributed by
Adrian Street Productions, P.O. Box 3514, Lubbock, TX 79452

Written & Edited by Dolores Mosser
Illustrations by Nathaniel P. Jensen
Executive Producer - Kerry Mosser
Image Editing & Book Production - Alan Klemp

The illustrations were rendered in watercolor on Arches paper.

ISBN: 978-0-615-31317-7

1 2 3 4 5 6 CP 14 13 12 11 10 09
Printed in The United States of America

To Adrian, Andrew, Ava, and Max,
this book is about the day Uncle Kelly
and I really saw a circus train.
I hope you never out-grow the fun of
watching trains go by, just like me!
– Dolores Mosser

For Mason and Tristan and all parents
of boys and girls who love trains.
– Nathaniel P. Jensen

"Mr. Jensen's creative illustrations give you lots to explore.
So, follow the red bird as he flies from page to page. I hope
this book brings you, your family and friends many years
of enjoyment. Thank you and read, read, read."
– D. Mosser

I live in a town where trains go by,
fast and slow we watch them go.
With flashing lights the guards go down
ringing bells, clacking sounds.

We stop the car and look outside
to see the trains go passing by.
So many trains go by each day,
I wonder which ones we will
see today.

6

Sometimes we see army trains,
sometimes we see trucks on trains,
sometimes trains with people inside,
sometimes just the engines go by.

10

The engine is in front, you know
it pulls the cars, to make them go.
Its horn is loud, we hold our ears,
be sure to wave at the engineer.

He's driving a freight train
and pulls out of our station.
Freight trains haul cargo
all over the nation.

The wheels go round, the cars roll by-
One car, two cars, three, four, five.
Box cars, tank cars, hopper cars, too.
Some flat cars, and look, at the end ...a caboose!

Can you say the color of each of the cars?
Do you see a red one, a blue one, green, black or orange?
From Alaska to Texas, California to Maine,
each freight train is different, they're never the same.

Lots of people ride on trains
to visit friends so far away.
They pack their bags
and climb on board
to travel safe from
shore to shore.

Through cities,

Through forests,

Cross wide, open plains.

The deserts,

Dark tunnels,

To the oceans,
Hooray!

They eat and sleep,
and look outside
as fields and
mountains hurry by.

Long trips or short,
in sunshine and rain,
it's fun to ride
on a choo-choo train.

My favorite one was a circus train
that came through town one summer day.
We watched and waited and to our surprise,
this special train did not pass by.

Instead it slowed
and soon it stopped,
a door popped open and then,

Guess What!

28

Out came a lion, a tiger, elephants by two,
a clown with a pony, the ringmaster, who
stopped to see us, and take in the view.
What a wonderful thing this traveling zoo!

A juggler, a zebra, a bear dressed in blue,
two seals, a lion tamer, and acrobats, too!
They thrilled us, amazed us, with all of their skills!
We even saw a clown walking high up on stilts!

The ringmaster waved his big hat,
and jumped back on the train.
The animals followed, the clowns did the same.

We waved from our car
and cheered with delight,
as this special train soon
vanished from sight.

34

Do you like to see trains
when you are out for a drive?
Do you like to count cars?
Or guess what is inside?

Then come with me now
and let's look down the tracks.
Perhaps that circus train
is on its way back!

A Train Story - Children's Activity Page

After you have read the story, go back through, page by page, and try to answer all the questions.

More questions and suggestions can be found at www.*atrainstory.com*.

Book Cover:
What is happening in this picture?
What sounds would you hear?

Intro. Page:
Where do you see the name of the town?
What does the flashing red light mean?

Pages 4 & 5:
What is the name of the street?
What kind of store is on the corner?

Pages 6 & 7:
The train moves along a t _ _ _ _.
Can you find the flag?

Pages 8 & 9:
Count the trains and say their colors.
What is on the green and yellow trains?

Pages 10 & 11:
What is the driver of the engine called?
How many people are in the yellow car?

Pages 12 & 13:
How many cars can you see?
Finds the logs? What's under the tarp?

Pages 14 & 15:
Find a cowboy.
The man in the blue uniform, what is he called?

Pages 16 & 17:
How are the city and forest different?
What animals do you see in the forest?

Pages 18 & 19:
Do the Plains have mountains?
What grows in the desert?

Pages 20 & 21:
Why do we need tunnels and bridges?
Can you find the beach?

Pages 22 & 23:
What is the boy handing to the conductor?
What do you see when you ride a train?

Pages 24 & 25:
How do we know it is a circus train?
Can you find a face on the engine?

Pages 26 & 27:
Can you find a monkey?
Can you count the wheels on the train?

Pages 28 & 29:
Can you find the Ringmaster?
Point to and say the names of all the animals.

Pages 30 & 31:
Are the people having fun? How do you know?
What sounds would you hear in this picture?

Pages 32 & 33:
How do we know the circus train is going to leave?
How many clowns can you find?

Pages 34 & 35:
Is the train leaving from or coming into town
Is the Conductor "on" or "off" the train?

Pages 36 & 37:
Add the number of children and adults together.
Are the children safe riding in the car? Why

Pages 35 & 36:
Did you enjoy seeing the circus train?
What did you like best?

Would you like to send us an email to info@atrainstoy.com.

You can write to us at:

A Train Story
P.O. Box 3514
Lubbock, Texas 79452

"Thank you for your attention and I hope you read this book many, many times."   -D. Mosser